CONTENTS

THE MAN-EATING MINOTAUR

Long ago, on the island of Crete, there lived the Minotaur. The one and only Minotaur. There has never been another. He was a most ferocious beast, half-man, half-bull, and he fed on human flesh.

4

King Minos, the ruler of Crete, kept
the Minotaur in a vast maze called the
Labyrinth, which had been specially built
underneath the royal palace. It was a
terrible place – so dark and such a mass
of twisting, turning passages that it was
impossible for anyone who went in ever
to find their way out again.

At that time, King Minos was all-powerful in the world of the Mediterranean, and in order to feed the ferocious beast he passed a grim law. It was this: every country, across the sea, must take it in turn to send, each year at springtime, seven lads and seven young girls, who would be thrust into the Labyrinth, one by one.

Eight years passed by, and the Minotaur was fed.

The ninth year came. It was spring. The sun shone, the birds sang and the almond trees were pink with blossom. But in Athens there was sadness. The time had come for the city to draw lots and choose seven lads and seven young girls and send them to Crete.

Now Aegeus, King of Athens, was an old man and very frail. But he had an only son called Theseus who was a handsome lad, tall, strong and fast on his feet. And the king loved his only son with a great love.

On the morning when the lots were to be drawn, the king, his son and the citizens of Athens gathered in front of the palace. Some were silent. Some wept.  Others whispered prayers to the gods: "Not my son! Not my daughter! Don't let them be chosen!"

When Theseus saw how sad everyone was, he said to his father, "I must go to Crete and try to kill this Minotaur!"

8

"No – don't go!" said the king. "It would mean certain death. You can't kill this beast alone and unarmed. And even if you did, you'd never find your way out of the terrible Labyrinth."

But Theseus turned to the crowd. "Lots will be drawn for only six young lads," he said. "I shall be the seventh. And, you can be sure, I shall try to kill the Minotaur!"

"Ohhhh…" There was a long, low gasp. Everyone was full of admiration that Theseus, the king's only son, should freely offer to go.

When the lots were drawn, and the seven girls and six lads chosen, Theseus gathered the young people round him. "Be brave," he said. "Always have hope. The Minotaur can't live for ever!" Then he led them down to the harbour, followed by their weeping mothers and fathers, sisters and brothers.

Just before Theseus boarded the ship that was to take him to Crete, King Aegeus put his arms about his son.

"Theseus, promise me one thing," he said. "The ship is rigged with the black sails of death. Now, if you are on board when it returns, take down the black sails and hoist white ones in their place. Then, even from a long way off, I shall know that you are alive and safe."

And Theseus promised.

A few days later, Theseus and his companions arrived at Knossos, the chief city of Crete. Armed guards met them and took them along steep paths, up stone steps and into the immense royal palace spread out high on a hill.

11

They entered a beautiful room where every wall was covered with bright painted pictures, and there, seated on his throne, was King Minos with his two daughters, Phaedra and Ariadne, on either side.

Thirteen prisoners stood with their heads bowed. Only Theseus stood,

straight and tall, and looked at King Minos, eye to eye.

"Bold youth," said the king, "who are you?"

"I am Theseus, son of Aegeus, King of Athens," he answered. "And I have come to kill the Minotaur so that no more of our young people need die!"

Then the king ordered the guards to search Theseus. And when they found that he carried no weapons, King Minos laughed. "How will you kill the Minotaur?" he asked. "With your hands?"

"If I must!" answered Theseus.

Ariadne, the princess, looked at Theseus. He was so brave, so strong. 'I will help him,' she thought. 'A man like this ought not to die!'

As soon as the young Athenians were taken away to the palace prison, Ariadne went to the kitchens and stirred sleeping powders into some large jugs of wine, and ordered servants to give the wine to the prison guards.

Then she went to her father's room and stole a fine sharp sword. Finally, she opened a small painted box in which she kept her private treasures and took out a ball of golden thread. This was the ball she had told no one about, not even her sister. It had been given to her when she was a little girl by clever Daedalus, the man who had designed and built the Labyrinth. He had said, "Play with the glittering ball, Ariadne. But don't forget. It has magic…" And he whispered something in her ear.

15

That night the guards, of course, slept *very* soundly! And so did the prisoners, who were tired from their journey. But Theseus lay awake, trying to work out how he could kill the Minotaur. About midnight the prison door swung open, and there stood Ariadne, the princess. "Come," she said. "Follow me."

She took him along winding corridors and down long stairways, down and down. At last she unlocked a heavy wooden door and opened it. In front of them was a narrow passage – and beyond it? There was darkness. They were at the entrance to the Labyrinth.

Then Ariadne gave Theseus her father's sword. "With this you can kill the Minotaur," she said. And then she gave him the ball of golden thread, but she held on to the loose end herself. "Place the ball on the floor," she said. "It will roll forward of its own accord, and guide you to the centre of the Labyrinth. When you return, wind it up and it will guide you out."

"And will you wait here till I return?" asked Theseus.

"I shall hold my end of the thread, and I shall wait!" said Ariadne.

Theseus placed the golden ball on the floor and, as it rolled off into the darkness, the threads glowed, giving out a hazy sort of light. He followed behind, along cold, narrow, stone passages. He turned to right and left, twisted back and turned again, on and on, following the ball.

He walked on until the golden ball came to rest in a large, grey, shadowy space. He had reached the heart of the Labyrinth, and there, as if waiting for him, was the Minotaur.

The ferocious beast swung his massive head from side to side. He snorted and stamped his feet. Then, lowering his shoulders, and with his horns, sharp as daggers, pointing forward, he charged.

Theseus gripped the sword and stood
his ground. The Minotaur was almost
upon him before, in one swift movement,
Theseus leaped aside,
turned and thrust
the sword into
the monster's
neck. It was
enough. The
beast stumbled,
slowly fell to the
floor, and died.

Now Theseus had to escape from the Labyrinth. He saw the golden ball shining hazily in a corner. He picked it up and set off, winding the thread round the ball as he went. And the thread led him, by the same twisting, turning route, back to the open door and Ariadne.

Then everything happened quickly. Theseus and Ariadne woke his young companions and guided them out of the palace, and on the way to the harbour Araidne decided to leave with them. She liked Theseus and wanted to be with him and, besides, she knew her father would be angry when he found out what she had done.

So they all boarded the Athenian ship,
the sailors were shaken till they opened
their eyes, and the black sails were
hoisted. Then – one final thing – before
they left Crete, Theseus and the young
lads set fire to King Minos's largest and
swiftest ships, in case the king chased
after them.

After a couple of days at sea a gale
blew up and the waves became wild and
choppy. Poor Ariadne was seasick and felt
so ill the only thing she wanted was to get
off the ship. As soon as possible!

She pleaded with Theseus, and in the
end he ordered the sailors to make for the
nearest island and put her ashore. Before
she stepped back on to dry land, Ariadne

and Theseus said fond farewells. But that was the end of their friendship. They never saw one another again.

Perhaps it was because of the rough seas and the upset of Ariadne leaving... who knows? Anyway, somehow, Theseus forgot his promise to his father, and he did not order the sailors to take down the black sails and hoist white ones in their place.

Day after day, old King Aegeus had watched from the top of the cliffs, waiting for the return of the ship that had taken Theseus to Crete. So, when one morning he saw a ship approaching, with black sails billowing in the wind, he thought his only son was dead. And, overwhelmed by sorrow, the king flung himself into the sea and drowned.

When Theseus's ship finally put down anchor, and he and the six lads and seven young girls came ashore, there was great joy in Athens.

"Theseus, our hero!" the people cried. "You have killed the Minotaur! You have saved our children!" And they hung garlands of flowers around his neck.

For a very short while Theseus was happy. But then a messenger arrived with news of his father's death. Theseus's eyes filled with tears. "The sails – the black sails!" he said. "Why did I forget?" But the deed was done. It couldn't be changed.

And then Theseus became King of Athens, and he was a good king, wise and strong, and loved by all his people.

But he never forgot his father, who had loved him with such a great love. In his honour, Theseus decided to call the sea where King Aegeus had drowned the Aegean. And so it has remained. Look on any map and you will find that the wide waters to the east of Athens are still called the Aegean Sea.

A Greek tale

THE
MAGIC FRUIT

In the time, long ago, when great and marvellous magicians lived on earth, Coniraya was the greatest. With his hollow stick he could flatten mountains. He could bring water to dry places. He could make magic that was big and strong. Yet, sometimes, because he liked jokes and pranks, he just looked around and made mischief.

Now while Coniraya was the greatest among magicians, there was a young woman called Cavillaca who was the most beautiful. She was so beautiful that every man, as soon as he saw her, wanted to marry her. But Cavillaca was proud. No living man was handsome enough or powerful enough for her. And so she refused to marry.

One day Coniraya was walking about the world disguised as a poor peasant, when he saw Cavillaca sitting under a tree, weaving. Then, like every other young man, he wanted to marry her.

"Greetings, beautiful Cavillaca," he said.

But Cavillaca kept her eyes on her weaving.

So Coniraya thought up some mischief. Next moment – there he was – a large bird with glorious rainbow-coloured feathers. He spread his wide wings and flew up to sit on a branch of the lucuma tree that stretched out above Cavillaca, and he began to sing.

But still she kept her eyes on the weaving.

Then Coniraya thought up some more mischief. He conjured up a fruit. A lovely ripe golden-orange fruit. And he hid some strong magic inside that fruit and dropped it straight down into Cavillaca's lap.

Well, the fruit looked so lovely, she had to pick it up. Then it smelt so good, she had to bite into it. And the taste was so delicious, she ate it to the last juicy mouthful.

She did not guess that it was a magic fruit.

33

Months passed by, and because of the magic fruit, Cavillaca had a son. He was a happy, smiling, beautiful baby, and she loved him with a great love. But she was curious and kept wondering who had made the magic and given her this baby...and how it had been done...and when. She thought about it and thought about it. When the baby was almost a year old and could crawl, she decided that she would find out who was the father of her beautiful child, and marry him, because, without doubt, he must be both exceedingly powerful and exceedingly handsome. So she summoned the great magicians to a meeting.

Of course, all the magicians came dressed in their most splendid robes, hoping that Cavillaca would notice them. All except for Coniraya, who was dressed, once again, in the torn, shabby clothes of a poor peasant.

The meeting began, and Cavillaca stood, proud and beautiful, with her baby in her arms. "Until this time I have always refused to marry," she said, "but now I solemnly promise that I will marry the father of my son, if he will make himself known to me."

But no one spoke. No one moved.

"If you will not speak, then my son shall tell me," said Cavillaca. "He will know his father and go to him." And she put the baby on the ground.

Immediately, he was off, crawling
eagerly straight towards the shabby
peasant. And when he reached the
peasant's feet, he looked up and stretched
out his arms.

Proud Cavillaca was angry.

"A poor peasant! No, I will *not* marry a
poor peasant!" she cried as she ran to the
baby and swept him up in her arms.
"Though I have given my promise," she
said, "I will *never* marry him. I would
rather die..."

And she clasped the baby close to her
and ran off.

37

"Stop!" Coniraya called out. "Stop! Things are not as they seem!"

But Cavillaca ran on and would not listen.

Then Coniraya struck the ground with his hollow stick. Next moment – there he was dressed in magnificent robes, dazzling and golden.

He called, "Beautiful Cavillaca, look back!

Turn your eyes towards me and see how handsome I have become!"

But she ran on.

And Coniraya was afraid of her stubborn pride and sorry for his own mischief-making, and he ran after her. But she heard him coming and gathered together her own powerful magic and hid herself from him and ran faster, faster, ever faster.

Though he could not tell where
Cavillaca had gone, Coniraya was
determined to find her. He ran and ran,
asking everyone he met if they had seen
her, but no one had. At last, good fortune
came, and he met the Condor who had
seen her and was able to show him the way.

Coniraya blessed the Condor. "I give you power to fly over the valleys and wild places, and to eat where you will," he said. "A curse be on those who kill the condor."

Coniraya ran on and more good fortune came. He met the Falcon who had also seen Cavillaca and was able to show him the way.

Coniraya blessed the Falcon. "I give you power to soar above the mountains," he said. "In song and dance people shall always praise the Falcon."

41

Coniraya ran on and again good fortune came. He met the Puma who was also able to show him the way.

Coniraya blessed the Puma. "I give you power over all other living creatures," he said. "At all times and everywhere people shall honour the Puma."

Coniraya ran on. He came to the sea. At last he saw Cavillaca. She was running across the sandy shore. He called to her, but she would not look back.

She gathered together her magic powers, and, holding the baby close in her arms, she plunged into the sea. Next moment – there was no beautiful Cavillaca and no baby. They were gone.

In their place stood two rocks, a large one and a small one close beside it. Two rocks and the waves gently lapping against them. That was all.

An Inca tale from Peru

THE MAN-EATING MINOTAUR

A Greek Tale

This Greek tale recalls some of the customs of an earlier civilisation ruled from the palace of Knossos in Crete. The first palace was built there nearly 4,000 years ago, but each time it was destroyed by earthquake or fire, another was built on top. In the ruins, many decorations celebrating bulls have been found – bulls' heads, horns and a wall-painting depicting the sport of bull-jumping. The acrobats, both young men and women, had to seize a bull by the horns, turn somersaults over its back and land on the ground behind.

The ancient Egyptian gods and goddesses often had a human body, with an animal head, such as a cat, a hawk, or like the Minotaur, a bull. Each god had the skills of the animal they resembled.

In *The Man-eating Minotaur*, Theseus is brave and strong. He volunteers to go to Crete, and there he kills the Minotaur. But he is so carried away by events that he forgets his promise to his father and does not put up the white sail. Proud Cavillaca, in *The Magic Fruit*, similarly does not keep a promise, and there is sadness at the end of both stories.

THE MAGIC FRUIT

An Inca Tale from Peru

In traditional magical tales things are not always what they seem, and the people who succeed are those who look beyond how someone is dressed or what they look like. In the French tale *Beauty and the Beast*, Beauty learns to love the ugly beast for himself and when she agrees to marry him she has no idea that he is really a handsome prince.

But Cavillaca, in *The Magic Fruit*, can only see a poor, shabby peasant, and she is so full of her own importance that she breaks her promise. She would rather die than marry Coniraya as she sees him. Foolishly, she neither listens nor looks back when he calls after her. Thus, Cavillica loses everything.

In this Inca tale, first written down by a Spanish settler in Peru, Coniraya and Cavillaca are 'huacas', the name given by the Inca people to spirits or gods who live in the world as humans. They used the word for other things that they thought were strange and magical too. Twins were 'huaca', as were the glass goblets that the Spanish brought with them when they settled in Inca territories.

MAGICAL TALES
from
AROUND THE WORLD

Retold by Margaret Mayo ✶ *Illustrated by Peter Bailey*

Orchard Myths are available from all good bookshops,
or can be ordered direct from the publisher:
Orchard Books, PO BOX 29, Douglas IM99 1BQ
Credit card orders please telephone 01624 836000
or fax 01624 837033
or e-mail: bookshop@enterprise.net for details.

To order please quote title, author and ISBN
and your full name and address.
Cheques and postal orders should be
made payable to 'Bookpost plc'.
Postage and packing is FREE within the UK
(overseas customers should add £1.00 per book).

Prices and availability are subject to change.